Rusty's Dilemma

– GREGOR GIRVAN –

www.fast-print.net/store.php

Rusty's Dilemma
Copyright © Gregor Girvan 2015

Illustrations by Ali Moreton.

A catalogue record for this book is available from the British Library

ISBN 978-178456-274-8

First published 2015 by
FASTPRINT PUBLISHING
Peterborough, England.

RUSTY'S DILEMMA

Bear words

groddle – human (man or woman)

grout – bad human

A New Day

Rusty walked from the training pitch with a huge grin on his face. He had just tricked Jimmy and scored with the last kick of the game. Jimmy came running over and put his arm around his team mate.

'Did you mean to put the ball through my legs or was it just lucky?' Jimmy enquired.

With a glint in his eye Rusty responded 'I'm afraid it was pure skill... helped, of course, by your bandy legs!'

Jimmy paused and then started laughing, 'I'll get you for that!' he exclaimed as they ran off the pitch.

Gasping for breath, Jimmy and Rusty entered the steamy changing rooms. Most of the other Ready Bears were in various states of dress either having finished their shower or about to start. There was lots of singing and as usual most of it was out of tune. AB was the loudest by far.

Suddenly the singing was interrupted as Jimmy took his usual pleasure in playing a tune from his bottom. It never ceased to amaze his team-mates that Jimmy possessed such trumping ability.

A hail of dirty clothes soon left Jimmy engulfed but with no embarrassment whatsoever, he grinned widely back at his team-mates.

Rusty chuckled to himself as he looked at the mess. He had come to know Jimmy quite well and liked his friend's happy-go-lucky nature. Together they gathered up the clothes and put them into the laundry bags.

Afterwards Rusty sat down and switched on his mobile. There was a text message to call his agent, Peter the Meeter, urgently. Rusty pressed the number and waited for the groddle to talk.

'Great news,' he said, 'the Balham Bears in London are interested in meeting you.' Rusty felt his fur stand on end.

'Are you there?' asked Peter the Meeter.

It was several moments before Rusty responded with a croaky 'yes.'

'They want to sign you, think of what that could mean,' urged the groddle.

'When is this meeting and what about my contract with The Ready Bears?' Rusty asked quietly.

There was a delay before the groddle responded. 'Don't mention this to anybody; let's wait until official contact has been made by the Balham Bears. Call me when this has happened, then we'll fix the meeting date.'

'Is it bad news'? asked Chi the captain, a giant panda, as he walked towards Rusty.

'No it's OK, no problem,' replied Rusty.

Making his way to the shower, Rusty was confused. He should have been happy but for some reason he felt flat.

As they were dressing after their showers, Luigi entered the changing room and approached Rusty.

'We need to have a chat,' said the coach.

'What about?' replied Rusty.

'It's a personal matter and best discussed in the office. I'll see you there in 15 minutes.'

As Luigi left, the rest of the Bears looked towards Rusty. This was an opportunity that AB couldn't resist. He rose to his feet and strolled over to Rusty.

'Who's been naughty, then...? Eating too much bamboo perhaps? Give me a hug and I'll check out your bear belly.'

The rest of the Bears howled with laughter as Rusty grinned and pushed AB away. He was used to such teasing and had grown to accept that it was part of being a Ready Bear.

The Opportunity

Rusty made his way along the side of the training pitches and through the car park. He entered the office building and took the stairs to the first floor. As he walked along the corridor, he passed one of the catering ladies.

'Hi Kate, how are you?'

'Just dandy,' she replied with a warm smile.

He liked Kate and the rest of the staff; they were friendly groddles and always appeared to have a genuine interest in the players' well-being. Rusty also knew that Kate had a soft spot for him especially when it came to serving up food as he always seemed to end up with more berries than any of the other Bears.

Rusty knocked on the coach's door and he heard Luigi shout, 'Come in.' Looking very serious behind his desk, Rusty tried to lighten the situation.

'Great work out today, looking forward to some glorious grub now.'

Luigi didn't respond and said somewhat sternly, 'Take a seat.'

Sitting in front of the desk, Rusty looked inquisitively at the coach.

'I'll come straight to the point,' said Luigi.

'We've had an approach from the Balham Bears, they want you to join them.'

With a deep intake of breath, Rusty asked in a quiet voice, 'What does it mean?'

'Well, the BBs have offered us a sizeable transfer fee and if you wanted to join them, the club would probably accept. There would be things to go through such as medical checks but they should be pretty straightforward.'

'But would you want me to leave?' asked Rusty.

'Certainly not,' replied Luigi.

'Of course the fee would be a great help to the club but at the end of the day, the decision is yours,' he continued.

Rusty knew the reputation of the Balham Bears, not only successful in England but they challenged regularly for cup competitions in Europe. He was also aware of their international fan base and that they were one of the richest clubs in the world.

'OK, I suppose I should speak to my agent,' replied Rusty reluctantly.

Luigi looked at Rusty, surprised that there hadn't been more of a reaction. He wanted Rusty to stay with The Ready Bears but the chance of playing for one of the biggest clubs in the world was surely an opportunity that he and most players would grab.

Getting up from his seat, Luigi put his arm over Rusty's shoulder.

'This approach is a great compliment and could be the biggest decision of your life,' said Luigi.

'What would you do if you were me?' asked Rusty.

Liugi paused for a few moments and said, 'My advice would be to go down to London and find out what's on offer... and whether the BBs are right for you. Take your time and speak to your friends and groddles you respect. Listen to them, not just your agent,' said Luigi gently.

Leaving the office, Rusty turned around and in a quiet voice, said, 'Thanks coach, I'll take your advice.'

Bright Lights.

A couple of days later, on the train to London, Rusty thought about his predicament. He loved playing for The Ready Bears and had never thought about leaving but no Bear would give up the chance to play football for the BBs, or would they?

Another thought passed through his mind. This trip would bring him into contact with many groddles. Rusty remembered the first time he had used his secret power and how he'd learned to control it. Rusty loathed evil groddles (grouts) especially those who treated others badly because of their skin colour or race; he wondered if he'd feel the need to use his power.

The train pulled into the station on time. Rusty walked briskly towards the taxi rank where he'd agreed to meet his agent.

'We're in good time for the meet,' said Peter the Meeter. 'I've given a tip off to some mates in the press, so there should be plenty of interest when we arrive.

Rusty looked at his agent and wondered why groddles' noses were so funny and didn't seem to work. Couldn't they smell themselves? he pondered.

Ten minutes later, Rusty climbed out of the taxi and was immediately surrounded by groddles with cameras.

There was much pushing and jostling but Rusty soon found himself in the grand stadium entrance of the Balham Bears. He was introduced to two groddles, one large and one small who remarked, 'First time we've had a red panda in here.'

Feeling very self-conscious and strangely alone, Rusty climbed the stairs to the first floor.

'Leave the talking to me,' whispered Peter the Meeter as they entered the boardroom.

A distinguished groddle shook Rusty's paw and for the next hour the groddles were locked in discussions. Rusty had soon become bored and he thought about the times he'd enjoyed with Jimmy and the other Ready Bears. His daydreaming was brought to an end when Peter the Meeter announced, 'Fine, we have the basis of a deal. We'll take the opportunity to meet the players and I just need to confirm a few things with my client.'

On the way to the Balham Bears' training ground, Peter the Meeter, was keen to finalise things.

'What a great meet,' he said loudly.

'Over double your current pay, luxury flat and lots of sponsorship deals. Hey, and what about the football? The BBs are one of the top ten teams in the world with facilities second to none. And whilst Glasgow's a great city, in comparison to London... well, chalk and cheese. I think you should sign up straight away. I'll arrange for the medical tomorrow and inform The Ready Bears.'

'Hold on,' replied Rusty. 'I've got to think about this – it's the biggest decision of my life.'

'What's there to think about? This is the best opportunity any bear could have,' said the groddle.

They arrived at the training ground and again Peter the Meeter did most of the talking. Rusty managed to have a conversation with several of the players but they seemed very serious and didn't appear to be interested in him. Furthermore, the way everyone was talking, it seemed as if the decision had already been made. Rusty decided to confront Peter the Meeter.

'I know you've put in a lot of effort but I'm returning to Glasgow tomorrow,' he said.

Peter the Meeter looked as if he'd just eaten a bumblebee sandwich. He blurted out, 'But what about the medical? Surely it would be good to meet the medical staff and make sure there aren't any problems?'

'No, I need a few days to think things over and to talk to my friends,' said Rusty in a determined voice.

Sitting in the waiting room at the train station, Rusty reflected on how everything seemed to have moved so fast. London's bright lights and sights seemed exciting but what about the new bears and groddles he'd met?

Rusty felt unsure.

Rusty Responds.

The waiting room door opened and two big white male groddles entered. They sat down and talked loudly. Soon afterwards they turned their attention towards a brown-skinned groddle sitting in the corner. For no apparent reason they started making rude remarks which then turned into insults. Not only was this bullying, it was an ugly attack on someone purely because they were a different colour. These weren't just groddles... they were grouts.

Rusty couldn't ignore the abuse and decided to speak up.

'That's enough!' he exclaimed.

The grouts both looked towards Rusty.

'It's none of your business... and you're only a bear or are you a raccoon?' one of them sneered.

Rusty knew there would be no reasoning with these grouts. He stared at the offenders and said slowly to himself, 'Bobble and wobble... be seen as green.'

The grouts started to scratch their skins and then stood up twisting in some discomfort. Both let out shrieks... and suddenly they stopped. The groddle in the corner looked on in astonishment. Rusty knew the change had been completed and opened the door to leave. As he looked back, the two green grouts stared at one another in bewilderment.

Rusty rarely used his power and only did so when he was sure that evil had been practiced. He knew that the two grouts would return to their original state after a couple of days but wasn't sure how they would act in the future.

What to do?

The next day, Rusty went back to training with The Ready Bears. As he entered the changing room the other Bears fell to their knees and bowed their heads.

'All praise the London Lord!' Jimmy cried out.

Rusty decided to play along with the tease. 'Each of you in turn, lick my feet,' he said jokingly.

'Left or right foot first?' asked AB.

Rusty laughed but couldn't continue with the joke.

'OK, OK, the Balham Bears only wanted to talk to me,' he exclaimed. 'They might want me to join them but I'm still a Ready Bear.'

'For how long?' asked Jimmy.

Before Rusty could reply, Luigi entered and shouted out 'finish changing and let's get moving, it's an important training session today.'

After the training had finished, Rusty spoke to Jimmy and AB about his dilemma. They clearly didn't want him to leave but couldn't imagine turning down an offer to join a club like the Balham Bears. Rusty decided to approach Chi. The Ready Bears captain was a great leader and although young, he was also very wise.

'Chi, can I ask your advice?' said Rusty. Chi smiled and they sat down together.

'I've met with the BBs and all sorts of benefits are being offered if I join them. Big car, lots of money, beautiful home... and then there's the facilities: new gym, treatment rooms, massive stadium... everything is so cool.'

'Sounds great,' replied Chi.

'But what do you think? asked Rusty.

'Well, you've mentioned some wonderful things but they are only things. If you're going to leave The Ready Bears, make sure you're doing it for the right reasons. Firstly, will moving to a richer club give you more opportunity to become a better player and be successful? Secondly, will you be happy playing for a different club, having new team-mates and working with other groddles? If the answer to both questions is yes, then you should leave. If however you think the answer to the first point is possibly yes but to the second point it's possibly no, then you have a head-or-heart decision to make.'

'I'm not sure I understand,' said Rusty 'can you please explain more?'

Well, if you feel the positives outweigh the negatives, it would suggest moving. On the other hand, if your internal feelings are telling you to stay and that is stronger, then that's what you should do. That is your dilemma. As for me, two years ago I turned down the chance to join the Beijing Bears. My heart ruled my head but as for you... only you know the strength of your internal feelings.'

Rusty's phone rang, it was Peter the Meeter.

'The BBs have agreed the transfer fee with The Ready Bears, so just the medical check and then you're a very rich bear.'

'But I haven't decided yet!' exclaimed Rusty

'But why would you stay with The Ready Bears?' barked the agent.

Rusty knew that Peter the Meeter would receive a large fee if the transfer went ahead and realised that he had a lot to lose if Rusty chose not to go. He decided to be courteous and replied, 'I've got lots to consider, thanks for your help, I'll call you back later with my decision.'

Rusty's Decision

Soon after, Rusty noticed that he'd been left a text message by Luigi who wanted to see him. The coach also wanted a decision.

Rusty slowly made his way to Luigi's office. His head was spinning. Fame and fortune or friends and fun? He thought he should leave, then he thought he should stay. How could he decide, what would help him make up his mind? Oh how he wished for something that would help him.

Heading towards the coach's office, he heard a voice behind him. 'Hi there' said Kate. 'I hear you're leaving us. It'll be so sad… you're one of the family,' she continued.

That was it, the decision was made. Rusty looked into Kate's eyes and without thinking, he replied, 'And how could I leave family? I'm afraid you'll be feeding me for a good few years to come.'

Kate beamed with joy and gave Rusty a groddle hug before rushing off to tell her colleagues.

Rusty felt relieved and suddenly very happy; instinctively he had made the decision and realised now what Chi had been talking about.

Rusty knew he had to speak to Peter the Meeter. He dialled the agent's number and was greeted with, 'Rusty the Balham Bear, sounds great, eh?'

'Well no, I prefer the Ready Bear and that's my decision.'

Furious with rage, Peter the Meeter shouted back immediately, 'You cur, you're nothing but a dog, a wimpering dog and so are all The Ready Bears!'

Rusty quite liked dogs and calmly replied, 'I understand you're upset and you don't mean to be insulting. '

'I do mean it!' shouted the agent.

Rusty could feel the hatred directed at him. Slowly he uttered... 'Bobble and wobble... hate become fate.'

Rusty heard a shriek and then a noise as the phone fell to the ground. There were a few moments of silence... and then... barking.

The Result

Six months had passed since Rusty's visit to the Balham Bears. Now he would meet them under different circumstances. As he ran onto the pitch at Blue Park, he felt rather strange but with a strong desire to play well. This was a cup game and to compete with the BBs was a huge match, particularly as The Ready Bears were the underdogs.

The crowd roared as The Ready Bears kicked off and Rusty felt his fur stand on end.

The first half was tough for Rusty and his team-mates as they spent most of their time defending. Only some great saves from Cool prevented the BBs from scoring. The second half continued in the same pattern with The

Ready Bears struggling to threaten the BBs goal.

As the game entered the final minutes, Jock made a good tackle and passed the ball forward to Rusty. Rusty saw a BB player approaching and pretended to go to the right side. When the player moved, Rusty pushed the ball through his legs and ran passed the bewildered bear. As a defender ran towards him, Rusty quickly glanced at the BBs' goal. He was far out and there were several bears in front of him. Rusty instinctively cut inside the defender and curled the ball towards the top corner of the goal.

Rusty saw the BB goalkeeper move quickly and leap to his left but it was to no avail. The ball glided passed his despairing reach and high into the net. The thunderous noise from the home supporters confirmed he'd scored.

Rusty found himself smothered by his team-mates and a few moments later he found himself in line with them doing The Ready Bears' hippy dippy celebration. The match lasted only a few more minutes and there were no more goals.

After the game, when Rusty was leaving Blue Park, he heard a voice behind him.

'Hi Rusty, tremendous win today.'

Rusty turned round and saw Peter the Meeter and with him was a small dog.

'I wanted to say sorry,' said the groddle. 'My behaviour in London was bad and I'd just like you to know that it won't happen again.'

'That's OK, I appreciate the apology' said Rusty. 'By the way, I thought you didn't like dogs,' he continued.

'Yes, that was the case but for some reason after our London trip, I took a liking to them,' said Peter the Meeter.

Rusty smiled and thought to himself, *Today's victory was great but the change in the groddle was an even better result.*

His special power had worked for the good.

A Trial for Iris

– GREGOR GIRVAN –

An environmentally friendly book printed and bound in England by
www.printondemand-worldwide.com

This book is made entirely of chain-of-custody materials